BLIND MAN'S BLUFF

Adapted by Sue Wright from the original episode

SCHOLASTIC INC.

New York   Toronto   London   Auckland   Sydney
Mexico City   New Delhi   Hong Kong   Buenos Aires

ISBN 0-439-69832-4

Copyright © 2005 Evangelical Lutheran Church in America.
Davey and Goliath ® and Davey and Goliath characters are registered trademarks of the Evangelical Lutheran Church in America.
All rights reserved.
Published by Scholastic Inc.
SCHOLASTIC and associated logos are trademarks and/or registered trademarks of Scholastic Inc.

Designed by Rick DeMonico

12 11 10 9 8 7 6 5 4 3 2 1   5 6 7 8 9/0

Printed in Singapore
First printing, February 2005

Sally opened the front door ready to scold her brother's dog. Goliath's sniffing and barking was driving her crazy!

Instead, she cried, "Come quick, Davey! Goliath's got the dog measles. He's so sick, he doesn't even know me."

After one look at the dog, Davey breathed a sigh of relief. "That isn't Goliath," he said.

"It certainly isn't," grumbled Goliath. "Get out of here!" he ordered the other dog gruffly. "You don't belong in this neighborhood."

"Why did you chase that dog away?" asked Davey. Goliath was usually polite to everybody, especially strangers.

"I didn't like his looks," said Goliath in a special voice he saved only for Davey.

"Gee, what a terrible reason!" exclaimed Davey. He was disappointed by his dog's behavior.

"But didn't you notice that dog was white with gray spots?" asked Goliath. "My fur is brown. Everybody knows brown dogs are better than white spotted ones."

Davey frowned. "Who convinced you of that, another brown dog? If you met that white spotted dog in a dark cave, you'd never know he wasn't the same color."

Goliath was glad when the telephone rang and
Mr. Hansen called out, "Jonathan for Davey!"
Davey started for the phone and then stopped.
"Tell him I'll be there in a few minutes, Dad."

"Shouldn't you move a little faster, Davey?" Goliath asked. "Jonathan Reed is your best friend."

"Not if I follow your rules," scolded Davey. "Have you forgotten? Jonathan and I are different colors. Jonathan is African-American and I'm white. According to you, I shouldn't take his phone call at all."

Goliath stared into Davey's face. He didn't know WHAT to think. "Davey," he moaned, "answer the phone!"

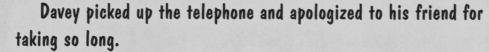

Davey picked up the telephone and apologized to his friend for taking so long.

"Are you too busy to talk?" asked Jonathan.

"I'm never too busy for my best pal," Davey answered. "What's up?"

"I want you to meet my cousin Scottie. Can you come over?"

"Sure," Davey replied. "I'll be there in half an hour."

"Are you headed for Jonathan's?" inquired Goliath.

"Yes, want to come along? He's introducing me to his cousin Scottie, though I have to admit, I don't understand why. Scottie's the boy who hates white kids."

"What kind of nut is that?" asked Goliath.

"Look who's talking!" hooted Davey.

"Thanks for getting here so soon," Jonathan whispered mysteriously. "We don't have much time."

"For what?" asked Davey.

"For teaching my cousin Scottie a lesson he can't seem to learn on his own," Jonathan declared.

"But how can I help, Jonathan? Scottie's the kid who said he'd never be friends with anybody white unless he was blindfolded and couldn't see the person was a different color."

"Correct, but listen to this!" Jonathan said. "Scottie's had an accident and has to wear bandages over his eyes for the rest of the week. This is our chance to prove to Scottie it's the boy and not his color that matters."

"Count me in," pledged Davey. "What's the plan?"

Jonathan explained that Scottie was staying with the Reeds until after the bandages on his eyes were removed. Jonathan wanted Davey to keep Scottie company while Jonathan worked at his father's drugstore. Once Scottie spent time with Davey, Jonathan felt sure Scottie would change his mind about hating all white kids.

"Oh, dear," groaned Davey, "that means Scottie has to like me or your plan will fail."

Jonathan left Davey and Goliath and returned with Scottie on his arm. "Here's my surprise," he announced to his cousin. "Scottie, meet my best friend Davey."

"And my dog, Goliath," answered Davey, trying not to sound too nervous.

Scottie reached out to pet Goliath. "What color is he?"

"Don't worry, he isn't white," said Jonathan.

"Please," begged Scottie, "no more lectures!"

Jonathan laughed. "It's a deal!"

"Tell me about your accident, Scottie," said Davey.

"I was in the attic using my brother's chemistry set, when all of a sudden, there was this huge explosion," Scottie said. "I blame it on my little sister. She swapped test tubes on me."

"My little sister does dumb things, too," said Davey.

"The attic filled up with the smelliest, thickest smoke you've ever seen," Scottie continued. "It got in my eyes and that's why I have to wear these bandages."

"The doctor doesn't want me messing with them," Scottie explained. "But I bet he wouldn't care if I lifted just one corner long enough to see what you and Goliath look like."

"Don't you dare!" squawked Davey.

"Okay, whatever you say, nurse!"

"Whew," exhaled Goliath, "ANOTHER experiment almost went *ka-boom*!"

Later that week, Mr. Reed and Pastor Miller stood in the drugstore window watching Davey and Scottie eat a snack at Pops' hot dog stand.

"Davey and your nephew seem to be making friends," observed Pastor Miller.

"Well, you can be sure it wouldn't be possible if it wasn't for those bandages on Scottie's eyes," Mr. Reed replied. "He had a run-in with one of his white classmates at school, and ever since, he's refused to be friends with anybody white."

While Davey spread mustard on Scottie's hot dog, Scottie brought Pops up to date on his week's activities. "Tomorrow I'm visiting at Davey's for the day and the next day he and I are going to Dr. Holmes to get my bandages off. Can you imagine any white kid being as nice as Davey?"

Pops gave Davey a knowing wink. "Maybe one," he answered.

That afternoon, Davey waited for Scottie to come over. "Have you got everything straight?" he asked Sally.

"Yes, Davey," she answered impatiently. "For the thousandth time, I'm not supposed to tell Scottie our family is pink."

"Not pink, Sally — white!" Davey exclaimed.

"But Davey, we aren't white. We're pink! Stop fretting. I'll keep your old secret."

"She's never kept one yet," said Goliath.

Soon, Davey was welcoming Scottie into the house and guiding him to the piano, where Sally still sat practicing. "Scottie, meet my sister, Sally," Davey said.

"Good to meet you," responded Scottie. "I can't see for myself, but Davey says I have a sister exactly like you."

"Well," tittered Sally, "not exactly. We're not the same...."

Anticipating Sally, Goliath began barking as loud as he could.

"Thanks, boy," Davey whispered. "You saved the day!"

"Anytime," Goliath replied. "But take my advice, Davey, if you want Scottie in the dark — keep him away from your little pink sister!"

The morning of his nephew's appointment
with Dr. Holmes, Mr. Reed telephoned the
doctor to ask him for a favor.

Dr. Holmes said he would be delighted
to cooperate.

Dr. Holmes was smiling as Scottie and Davey entered his office. "Excited about getting those bandages off?" he asked Scottie.

"I sure am," exclaimed the boy. "You said I'd be seeing as clearly as I was before the accident."

The doctor chuckled. "You might see even better." Then he asked Davey to step into the waiting room while Scottie's bandages were being removed. He would bring Scottie to Davey once Scottie was seeing all right again.

Or, Davey stewed to himself, *all wrong.*

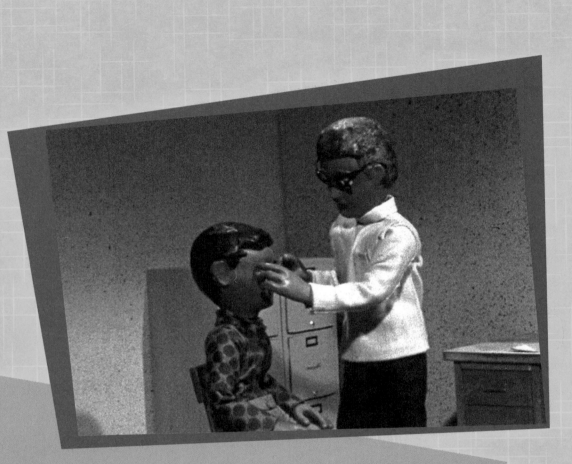

"Your vision may be fuzzy in the beginning,"
advised Dr. Holmes, "but don't panic, Scottie. After
your eyes have adjusted, everything will come into
focus. Now, let's get those bandages off. Enough of
this blind man's bluff!"

As the doctor predicted, everything did appear fuzzy at first. But after Scottie blinked his eyes a few times, his sight was nearly perfect.

"Hooray," Scottie cheered, "I'm my normal self again."

The instant Scottie saw Goliath in the waiting room, he ran to give the dog a hug. "I'd know you anywhere," he whooped. "But where's Davey?"

Davey found himself unable to speak. But Goliath's wagging tail and the slobbery kiss he slathered across Davey's face revealed the truth.

"You're Davey?" exclaimed Scottie. "But you can't be — you're white!"

"Not me," sputtered Davey. "I'm pink. At least, that's what my little sister says."

"You're white and you know it!" Scottie shouted. "You and Jonathan have been trying to fool me."

"Jonathan and I have been trying to help you, Scottie," Davey protested.

"I don't need your kind of help, Davey Hansen."

That afternoon, Davey was upset about losing Scottie as a
friend. So he dropped by Goliath's doghouse for a chat.
"I guess some folks will never learn to be color-blind,"
Davey remarked sadly.

"Perhaps some won't, Davey, but thanks to you, I have," said Goliath.

Davey looked around at Goliath in wonder. "You have?"

"I have indeed. Meet my new friend, Spots."

The moment Davey saw the dog Goliath had chased from the Hansens' house just days before, his spirits lifted. "At least I know a dog that's changed his mind," Davey said.

"You know a boy who's changed his, too."

Davey couldn't believe his ears. It was Scottie!

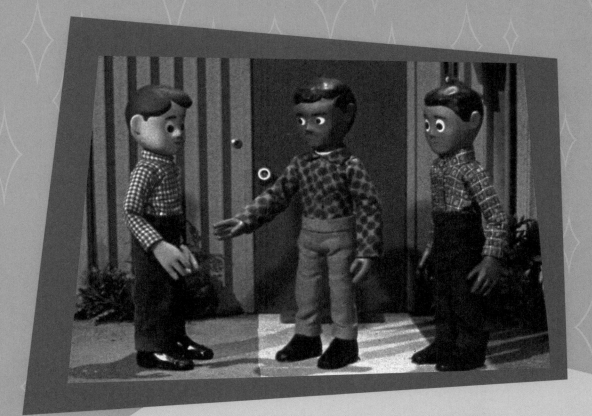

"Nurse, can we be friends again?" Scottie asked.

"Of course," exclaimed Davey. "That's all Jonathan and I ever wanted."

"I understand that now," said Scottie, "but at the doctor's office, I still had smoke in my eyes."

"I used to have smoke in my eyes, too," confessed
Goliath, "but now, all I see is Spots!"

The End